A Silly SCIENCE Experiment

Thanks, Gina Shaw, for your input
and contagious enthusiasm!

—T.R.

ISBN-13: 978-0-545-00400-8
ISBN-10: 0-545-00400-4

12 11 10 9 8 7 6 5 4 3 2   7 8 9 10 11 12/0

Printed in the U.S.A.
First printing, November 2007

COMIC GUY™

A Silly SCIENCE Experiment

BY TIMOTHY ROLAND

Scholastic Inc.
New York Toronto London Auckland Sydney
Mexico City New Delhi Hong Kong Buenos Aires

CHAPTER ONE
A SUPER BLOOPER START

Last week's science class was a *real* blast. That's because Miss Lizzy tried one of her crazy experiments, which resulted in…

—an explosion

—an evacuation

—major repairs to our fifth-grade classroom.

But she promised that this week something even bigger would happen. Which is why I should have run for the hills. But I stayed, hoping I'd get some ideas for my comic strip. And hoping I'd survive.

By Monday morning, everything was back to normal in the science room. The hole in the ceiling had been repaired. The walls had been repainted. And everyone sat on the edge of their seats, wondering what our nutty teacher would do next.

Except for me.

I was working on a **COMIC GUY** comic strip. I write and illustrate the strip for the school newspaper. It's about me, and about what happens at school.

"Great idea, Guy," said Molly, my best friend, as she looked over at my comic strip. "I wish I had brought my helmet."

"Me, too," I said.

We both laughed. Then we watched as Miss Lizzy dashed into the classroom. "I wonder what we'll be doing this week," whispered Molly.

"There's only one way to find out," I whispered back.

Miss Lizzy wrote the word "STARS" on the board, then turned to face the class. Immediately, Molly's hand shot into the air. "Are we going to study stars this week?" she asked.

"No," replied Miss Lizzy.

WE'RE GOING TO BE STARS!

She looked at our confused faces. Then she cracked a goofy grin, hopped on top of her desk, and took off her white lab coat. Underneath, she was wearing a costume—with boots, a skirt, a long cape, and a shirt with a large yellow *S* on the front.

"What's she doing?" asked Molly.

I couldn't answer, because I couldn't believe my eyes.

Especially when I watched our science teacher leap from her desk and land in a heap on the floor.

"So tell me," said Miss Lizzy as she wobbled to her feet, "what did I just demonstrate?"

"That you're a nut," whispered Molly.

I chuckled.

Miss Lizzy straightened her hair and scanned the class. "What I demonstrated," she explained, "was gravity, the force of nature that pulled me to the ground."

I quickly waved my hand in the air.

"Yes, Guy?" asked Miss Lizzy.

"I don't understand."

"Gravity?"

"No," I said. "I don't understand why you didn't fly instead of fall. Aren't you... Superwoman?"

Everyone cracked up.

Miss Lizzy cleared her throat, then grinned. "That's a logical conclusion,  Guy," she said, pointing to the *S* on her shirt.

"But it's wrong. Because I'm not Superwoman. I'm...Sciencewoman!"

"Sciencewoman?"

"Have you ever seen *The Super Science Show* on TV?" asked Miss Lizzy.

The show, which stars Super Stan the Scienceman

— demonstrates science
— makes me laugh
— helps me learn
— is one of my favorite shows.

"Of course I've seen it," I replied.

"Well, Super Stan is leaving the show," explained Miss Lizzy. "And they've asked me to try out to take his place."

"What?!" roared Tank. The room shook as the class bully jumped to his feet and shot our teacher a worried look.

"Because—" Tank's mouth hung open for a moment as everyone turned and stared. Then his cheeks grew red and a scowl crept onto his face as he slowly lowered his huge body back onto his chair.

"What's with him?" whispered Molly.

"Beats me," I replied before looking again at Miss Lizzy.

"As I was saying," she continued, "on Thursday, I will be hosting the show and teaching about gravity to a worldwide TV audience."

"Wow!" I gushed. "You're going to be a star!"

Miss Lizzy's eyes sparkled. "You mean, *we're* going to be stars. Because you are going to be part of the TV show, too!" She pointed her finger at the class and smiled.

Everyone smiled back.

Except for Tank.

STAY TUNED FOR THE WHOLE SILLY STORY.

CHAPTER TWO

STARRING...ME?

Actually, I was already a star.

I was the star of my comic strip, **COMIC GUY**. Someday it will be printed in every newspaper in the world. But at the moment, it appears

only in our school newspaper. And everyone at Rockyville Elementary School loves it.

Well, everyone except...

Zoe.

SHE'S A BRAIN.

SHE'S A CRAB.

SHE'S THE EDITOR
OF THE SCHOOL
NEWSPAPER.

She wanted the newspaper to be more
serious. She wanted to get rid of **COMIC
GUY**. But she couldn't, because **COMIC GUY**
was the paper's most popular feature.

So I was a star—a comic strip star. And
according to Miss Lizzy, I was about to
become a TV star.

"If your project passes the test," she added.

"What project?" I asked. "And what test?"

Miss Lizzy grinned. Then she stood in front of the class and scanned our puzzled faces.

"Tonight, class," she said, "you are to read chapter three in your science textbook. Then, tomorrow, in groups of two, I'd like you to prepare an exciting demonstration on the subject of gravity."

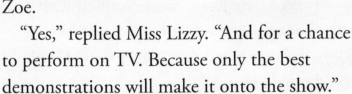

"For a grade?" asked Zoe.

"Yes," replied Miss Lizzy. "And for a chance to perform on TV. Because only the best demonstrations will make it onto the show."

"But what if none of them are good enough?" asked Tank with a sneaky grin.

"What do you mean?" asked Miss Lizzy.

"What if...somehow...they all flop?"

Miss Lizzy grinned. "That's not going to happen. Not with my students, who, like always, are going to do their very best."

"To mess things up," chuckled Tank softly.

I glanced at his shifty eyes, then back at Miss Lizzy.

"Because not only does *The Super Science Show* need a new host," she explained with a grin, "but they'd also like to add someone to their regular student cast." She pointed at the class. "Maybe you."

"You mean," beamed Zoe, "that one of us could be a permanent TV star?"

Miss Lizzy nodded.

Everyone's eyes (except Tank's) widened. And

they smiled. And they pictured themselves as stars.

But it wasn't going to happen. Because only one person was going to be chosen. And that person was going to be...

ME.

THE BARKER

Rockyville Elementary School News

KIDS SEE STARS

Miss Lizzy's students will compete for a chance to appear on TV. "Those who come up with the best experiments," explained Miss Lizzy, "will perform them on Thursday's *The Super Science Show*."

"Which means that although I'll be demonstrating gravity," explained Guy Maloney, "I hope what everyone sees is a star."

CHAPTER THREE
(ALMOST) TOGETHER

Monday night I read the chapter on gravity in my science book. And by Tuesday morning, I was so eager to get to school that I...

Fell out of bed.   Knocked over a lamp.

Stumbled down my porch steps.

 Molly and I laughed as we headed to school. We are neighbors and best pals. And like gum on a sneaker, we always stick together.

"After our class appears on TV," said Molly, "who do you think the show's director will pick to be the new cast member?" She flashed me a TV star smile.

I paused for a moment, pretending to think. "Hmm. He'll probably pick—"

"No. Me."

"No. Me!" Molly's cheeks reddened and her eyes tightened into angry slits as she stepped closer.

"Of course," I said, "if we don't come up with a science project that Miss Lizzy likes, it won't matter. Because we won't even get to be on the TV show!"

Molly's scowl softened. "You're right," she said. "Do you have any ideas?"

"Not yet."

"Me, neither."

"But if we put our heads together," I said, "we'll definitely come up with a great science project. And do you know why?"

Molly looked at me funny.

"Because we're a great team!"

We both grinned. And we smacked our right hands together. And we smacked our left hands together. Then we headed into our science room to see what everyone was working on.

DID YOU COME UP WITH AN EXPERIMENT ON GRAVITY, CLINT?

YEP. THANKS TO GRAVITY.

I JUST THREW SOME IDEAS INTO MY HEAD.

AND EVERYTHING FELL TOGETHER.

GUY MALONEY

TIFFANY SAYS SHE'S READY FOR THE MOST IMPORTANT PART OF APPEARING ON THE SHOW.

BECAUSE SHE CAME UP WITH A GREAT SCIENCE PROJECT?

GUY MALONEY

BECAUSE I'LL LOOK GOOD ON TV.

YOU THINK TANK CAME UP WITH A SCIENCE PROJECT?

YOU THINK HE CAN READ?

YOU THINK WE CAN OUTRUN HIM?

GUY MALONEY

DID YOU THINK OF AN EXPERIMENT YET, ZOE?

ACTUALLY, I'M EXPERIMENTING RIGHT NOW TO SEE IF I CAN GET RID OF PEOPLE WHO ASK ME STUPID QUESTIONS.

IT WORKED.

GUY MALONEY

YOU TWO ARE GOING TO BE PARTNERS, ZAPPER?

YEP. I'M GOING TO MAKE A SCIENTIST OUT OF OLLIE.

OR HE'S GOING TO MAKE A MONKEY OUT OF YOU.

GUY MALONEY

Ollie, of course, is the science classroom pet. So are Iggy (a shy iguana) and two hamsters, Peanut and Popcorn. And in what she calls an experiment, Miss Lizzy lets them all roam outside of their cages.

"And now, class," announced Miss Lizzy, "it's time for another experiment."

The room grew quiet.

I stopped working on my comic strip and listened as our teacher explained further. "You will prepare an experiment demonstrating gravity.

 The best ones will be chosen for the TV show. You will be working in groups of two."

I flashed Molly a thumbs-up sign. She flashed one back.

"And," continued a smiling Miss Lizzy, "to mix things up a bit, I will pick the groups."

My mouth dropped open. "What?"
"Zapper and Tiffany," said Miss Lizzy.
"What?"
"Molly and Clint."
"WHAT?"
"Guy and…"

CHAPTER FOUR

EEEK!

It was like being served the cafeteria's mystery meat stew …for three days in a row!

Or like being flooded with tons of homework…on the day before a vacation!

It was BAD NEWS!

BUT MOLLY AND I ARE ALWAYS PARTNERS.

WELL, THIS TIME THINGS ARE GOING TO BE DIFFERENT.

THIS TIME YOU WILL TEAM UP WITH ZOE.

WHO CERTAINLY IS DIFFERENT.

And that's why I call Zoe a queen bee. Because she likes to be in charge. Because she likes to boss people around. Because when irritated, she likes to attack . . . and sting.

I had to be careful. But I also had to get onto the TV show. Which was why I followed Zoe to her desk.

"It's my experiment, too!" I told her.

"So?" She flipped open her notebook.

"So...I want to be part of it."

"Do you?" Zoe looked down at her notes. She looked over at me. Then an evil grin slithered onto her face.

HMM. MAYBE I CAN USE YOU.

"What do you mean, 'use me'?" I asked.

"You'll see."

"When?"

"Soon." She glanced at me like she was my boss. Like she was in total control, until—

"EEEK!"

Zoe's eyes popped open. Her face turned

white. She pointed at the wiggly rodent clawing its way up her trembling arm.

It was definitely an emergency situation. So I lunged to the rescue. I grabbed the crazy critter. I hoisted him into the air. Then I looked at Zoe. "What are you trying to do?" I asked. "Scare Peanut to death?"

"Ha! Very funny!" Zoe's face turned red as she stared at our classroom pet.

"Get him away from me!" ordered Zoe.

"Here. I'll take him," said Tank, who stepped from behind me and grabbed hold of Peanut. "We're doing an experiment. And we have a few more kids to scare...I mean, to visit."

I watched Tank flash an evil grin, then walk away. "I wonder what he's up to?" I asked.

"Who cares!" snapped Zoe. She flipped open her notebook and shot me a bossy stare.

NOW, LET'S GET TO WORK!

CHAPTER FIVE

HERE'S THE PLAN...

I wasn't in a good position to argue (at least, not if I wanted to survive until the show). Instead, I asked, "So what are we going to do?"

"First," replied Zoe, "I'm going to think." She pulled out her notebook.

I flipped open my science textbook to the chapter on gravity, hoping I could help. I knew gravity was the force of nature that pulled things toward the Earth. "So to demonstrate gravity," I suggested, "we could—"

DROP A BALL.

FALL OVER.

JUMP OFF A DESK.

"That's all kid stuff," said Zoe, while sticking her nose in the air.

"Well, in case you haven't noticed," I said, "we *are* kids."

"Hmph," mumbled Zoe. "Maybe *you* are."

"So what are we going to do?" I asked.

"Demonstrate air resistance." Zoe slid a chair toward me. "Here, Guy, stand on this."

"Why?"

"Just do it!"

"But—" I glanced at Zoe's fiery glare. Then,

slowly, I stepped onto the chair. I am afraid of heights, and although the chair was close to the ground, I felt a little dizzy.

"Here." Zoe handed me two rubber balls, one with a small parachute attached. "The parachute will hit lots of air when it opens and slow down gravity's pull," she explained. "Now drop both balls!"

I did. But the parachute didn't open. And the two balls hit the floor at the same time.

"Hmm." Zoe looked at the chair. Then she grabbed my arm, and before I knew it, she had pulled me down the hall and we were standing in front of the janitor's supply closet.

"What can I do for you kids?" asked Mr. Ralph, the school janitor, as he opened the door and invited us in.

"We need a ladder for Guy to climb," replied Zoe.

"We do?" My stomach did a quick flip-flop.

Mr. Ralph chuckled and pointed toward the wall. And for a moment, I felt like Goldilocks as I examined the ladders.

"We'll take the biggest one," said Zoe.

I looked at her. I looked at the ladder. Then I almost threw up.

"Actually," said Mr. Ralph, "climbing up and down a tall ladder is easy, if you remember one thing."

"What's that?" I asked.

"Don't look down." Mr. Ralph winked and cracked a grin. Then he helped me carry the ladder to the science room, where I was about to find out if he was right.

CHAPTER SIX

HOW ABOUT THIS?

When we arrived back in the science room, Zoe handed me the two balls (one with and one without a parachute). Then, as I climbed the ladder, I followed Mr. Ralph's advice.

And it worked! I didn't get wobbly. Or dizzy. Or sick. And when I reached the top, I smiled a little to celebrate my accomplishment. Then, I dropped the balls (without looking down).

"Success!" yelled Zoe. "The parachute opened, and they hit the floor at different times!"

"They did?" I asked.

"Yes. Now get down here!"

I took a deep, calming breath. Then, carefully (and slowly), I climbed down each step of the ladder until I was standing on solid ground again.

"What do you mean our experiment's not exciting enough?" I asked.

"It's too ordinary," replied Zoe. "We need to

find something more interesting to drop."

"Oh," I said as I looked around. "How about...apples?"

"No. Too dull."

Zoe glared at me. "Get serious, Maloney, and think! We need something entertaining, something lively."

"Like what?" I looked at Zoe, then scanned the room again, hoping to spot something we could use in our experiment.

And I did.

It was wiggly. It was furry. And it was racing straight toward Zoe's leg.

CHAPTER SEVEN

SUCCESS!

"No, I'm not," I said. "It's a great idea."

"It's a dumb idea!" Zoe glanced down at me and pointed at Peanut. "Because I'll never do anything with that stupid rat! Never! Ever!"

"But he's not a rat," I said. "He's a hamster."

"I don't care!"

"And he's exactly what you said you wanted—something entertaining and lively."

"Hmph!"

"And using him will make ours the best and most exciting experiment. Which will definitely get you noticed by *The Super Science Show*'s director, the person looking to add someone to the TV show's permanent student cast."

Zoe's eyes widened. "You really think so?"

"Of course."

USING A HAMSTER IN OUR EXPERIMENT WILL MAKE IT FUN AND EXCITING.

AND UNPREDICTABLE.

WHICH IS WHAT WILL MAKE IT FUN AND EXCITING.

"Will I have to touch him?" asked Zoe.

"Nope."

She shifted her eyes from Peanut to me. "But we need two things to drop. And both need to be the same size and weight."

"No problem." I raced to the hamster cage, grabbed a rubber toy hamster, and brought it to Zoe. "So what do you think?"

a real
hamster

a fake
hamster

a real
smile

a fake
smile

Zoe looked at the toy, then looked at Peanut. "I'm still not sure it will work."

"Well, there's only one way to find out," I said as I quickly prepared Peanut.

HELMET
To protect
his head.

PARACHUTE
To slow
his fall.

GRIN
Which shows he has no idea
what is about to happen.

Then, without looking down, I began to climb the ladder with Peanut in my hand. And that's when he went wild.

"Maybe he's afraid of heights," I said as I stepped back on the ground.

"Or maybe," said Zoe, "this is a stupid idea."

"Or maybe he needs some of this," said Tank, who stepped from behind me holding a slice of—

"Pizza?" I said.

"Yep. He's crazy for it. See." As Tank held it closer, Peanut went wild. "But when he eats some," said Tank as Peanut leaped from my hand onto the slice, "he calms down."

"Thanks for the help, Tank," I said, somewhat surprised.

"My pleasure." He handed me the calmed-down hamster, then flashed a sneaky grin as he walked away.

"But what's going to stop Peanut from going crazy and running wild when he lands?" asked a nervous-looking Zoe.

"This." I moved Peanut's cage to the bottom of the ladder. "When I drop him, he'll land in here."

"Hmm. Let's try it," said Zoe. She motioned for me to climb the ladder with both the toy and the real hamster. Then, after rambling through her speech explaining our demonstration, she yelled, "Now, Guy!"

I dropped the hamsters.

"Perfect!" yelled Zoe as I climbed down to the floor. "They landed at different times. And," she said while pointing at the parachute-covered hamster in the cage, "he passed the test."

"And so did you," said Miss Lizzy as she stepped closer. "Both of you."

"You mean, we get A's?"

"Yes." Miss Lizzy's eyes twinkled. "And tomorrow, you will perform your experiment on TV."

CHAPTER EIGHT

Performing our experiment was easy for Zoe. She got to stand at the bottom of the ladder and explain what was happening—while I got stuck doing all the hard stuff!

Fortunately, Miss Lizzy had already chosen me and Zoe to be on the TV show. So I could relax for a moment and watch the others go through their experiment tryouts.

THE ONLY WAY
TO ESCAPE
EARTH'S GRAVITY
IS TO GET
FAR AWAY.

LIKE ON A
ROCKET...
OR ON A
SATELITE...

OR —

GUY MALONEY

ASTRONAUT

ASTRO<u>NUT</u>

GUY MALONEY

THE FASTER I GO...

THE FARTHER I FLY.

CRASH!

AND THE HARDER I FALL.

GUY MALONEY

MOLLY'S JUMP, LADIES AND GENTLEMEN, DEMONSTRATES THE EFFECT OF GRAVITY.

AND THE RESULT OF LEAPING BEFORE THINKING.

GUY MALONEY

List of experiments
Miss Lizzy picked to
be on the TV show.

THE BARKER

Rockyville Elementary School News

STARS CHOSEN

Miss Lizzy picked the students who will perform experiments on tomorrow's *The Super Science Show*. "And the show's director will pick one of us to be a regular cast member," said Guy. "So our experiment has to be perfect."

"You mean," stated Zoe while practicing her TV star smile, "it has to be better than perfect."

WHEN WE DO OUR EXPERIMENT ON TV, GUY...

THINK!

AND BE CAREFUL!

AND DON'T MESS UP!

OR MAKE ME LOOK BAD!

OR ELSE!

AND SMILE.

GUY MALONEY

CHAPTER NINE
DOUBLE TROUBLE

Thursday was show day. And I was ready.
Almost.

When the bus arrived at school, I loaded it with the stuff for our experiment. "Do you have everything?" asked Zoe.

"We have Peanut," I replied. "And the toy hamster. And the parachute."

"And where's the ladder?"

"Oh…right… the ladder." My knees shook as I stared at it sitting in the school hallway. Then, with Mr. Ralph's help, I loaded it onto the bus.

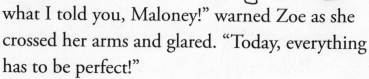

"Remember what I told you, Maloney!" warned Zoe as she crossed her arms and glared. "Today, everything has to be perfect!"

"But—"

"So now do we have everything?"

"Yes," I said as I looked at Peanut jumping around in his cage. "Everything, except—"

"Except what?"

"I'll be right back," I said. I turned and raced to the kitchen. Unfortunately, there was no leftover pizza for me to feed to Peanut. So I raced back into the hallway, but didn't get very far before I ran into—

"About what?" I asked.

"About the TV show. And about Miss Lizzy."

"She's perfect for the part of Sciencewoman."

"I know," said Tank. "And that's the problem. Because if she gets the job on the TV show, she's going to leave our school."

"Oh…right." I looked at Tank's worried face. "Hey, wait a minute. I thought you didn't like teachers."

"Well, I like Miss Lizzy," said Tank as a rare smile stretched across his face. "She's fun. And she makes me believe that even I can be a good student, if I try."

I smiled, too. "Yeah. She's the best teacher we have."

Tank nodded. Then he glared. "And if she leaves, you know who the school will probably get to replace her?"

I pictured in my mind the type of teacher we could get.

STRICT

NEXT ONE WHO BREATHES, GETS IT!

CRABBY

STOP BOTHERING ME WITH YOUR STUPID QUESTIONS!

BORING

FOR THE NEXT THREE HOURS, I WILL EXPLAIN THE FIRST PARAGRAPH OF YOUR TEXTBOOK'S CHAPTER ON GRAVITY.

TOUGH

HERE'S TONIGHT'S HOMEWORK ASSIGNMENT.

"So we have to make sure Miss Lizzy doesn't get the job," said Tank, "by messing up the show…by messing up our experiments."

"Are you kidding?" I said. "I can't do that. You know what Zoe would do to me if that happened?"

"But you've got to," said Tank as he shook his fist in front of my face.

Fortunately, just then Miss Lizzy zoomed toward us.

I followed her out the doorway and onto the bus. When I stepped inside, I was yanked onto a seat by Zoe. "You better be ready, Maloney,"

she snarled. "Because our experiment needs to be perfect!"

"I am." I leaned back against the seat and sighed. "At least I think I am."

"Why? What's wrong?"

"Nothing," I said softly. Although at the moment I had no idea what I was going to do.

CHAPTER TEN
READY OR NOT

When we arrived, Zapper helped me carry the things for my science experiment into the studio building.

Actually, I was hoping Zoe would change into

a less crabby person. But when she returned, she was wearing a brand-new pink dress.

Brand-new dress, but same old Zoe.

"Is everything ready?" she asked.

"Yep," I replied.

"And the cage is in exactly the right spot?"

"Yep." I watched her nervously look at the hamster, then at me. "Don't worry," I said.

"Don't worry?! For me to be picked for the show's cast, our experiment has to be perfect! And I have to be perfect!"

"Why don't you relax and just do your best?"

Zoe looked at me, at the hamster cage, at the ladder. Then her eyes popped open. "I can make our experiment better!" she gushed.

"How?" I watched Zoe smile, spin around, and push her way into the crowd. Then I heard a funny noise coming from the hamster cage. I turned and saw—

Peanut ramming the side of his cage.

Tank grinning.

CLINK! CLINK! CLINK!

Between the two was Tank's experiment, which had a smell that was driving Peanut crazy.

WHAT'S UNDER THERE?

YOU'LL SEE.

WHEN?

LATER.

WELL, GET IT OUT OF HERE! IT'S DRIVING PEANUT CRAZY!

I KNOW.

YOU DO?

Tank's beady eyes shifted back and forth. "I've got a plan for keeping Miss Lizzy at our school."

"You already told me," I said. "But I can't help you do it. Because it wouldn't be fair to Miss Lizzy for us to mess up the TV show."

"And it wouldn't be fair to us for her to leave!" growled Tank as he stepped closer.

"Well," I said, "I'm not going to goof up my experiment."

Tank glared at me for a moment. Then he grinned like a sneaky crocodile, picked up his bag-covered experiment, and carried it across the TV soundstage.

I watched Peanut finally calm down. Then I leaned against the ladder and wondered what

Tank was planning. And I worried a little—
until Zoe returned with an even taller ladder.

Then I worried a lot.

CHAPTER ELEVEN
A SMELLY SURPRISE

"Take your places!" yelled the director. "The show is about to begin!"

Everyone rushed off the stage. The room grew quiet. But it was still noisy inside my head.

The show started with a BOINK!

The director yelled, "Action!" Then Miss Lizzy walked into the spotlight, smiled, and—

BOINK!

was hit on the head by an apple. She rolled her eyes, wobbled, and fell to the floor as everyone laughed.

"Some say that's how gravity was discovered," she said as she looked into the camera. "That it happened when a guy named Newton was beaned by a falling apple." She picked up the apple and took a bite.

"Of course," she continued, "Newton didn't actually discover gravity. But he did observe how it behaves."

I watched Miss Lizzy smile and pick up two rubber balls. She was a great teacher and would make a great Sciencewoman. I felt happy for her. Then I felt an elbow jab me in the back.

"He's going crazy," whispered Zoe.

"Who?"

"Peanut. Look!"

I turned and saw Tank rushing away. Then I saw his bag-covered experiment within smelling distance of the hamster cage. Inside, Peanut was bouncing off the walls, trying to attack the experiment.

"What's wrong with him?" asked Zoe.

"Nerves," I lied.

I held Peanut's nose. He calmed down. So I took him with me as I returned to watch Miss Lizzy perform.

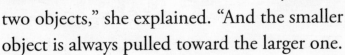

"Gravity is the attraction between two objects," she explained. "And the smaller object is always pulled toward the larger one.

Like us toward the Earth."

74

The lights dimmed. The cameras swung toward the other side of the stage—toward Tank!

"Balance is determined by gravity," he explained. "And to stay balanced, the center of our weight—called our center of gravity—must be over the top of our base, which is our feet."

I stared for a moment, then rubbed my eyes.

Tank grinned. Then he yanked the plastic bag off his experiment. It was a tower made from dozens of slices of pizza!

"That's why it drove Peanut crazy," I whispered.

Tank's grin widened. He pulled on a piece of string and his tower began to tilt. "Shift the center of gravity off its base, and my building falls," he said. "But shift it only a little, so it's still over its base, and the building becomes—the Leaning Tower of Pizza!"

Everyone laughed, including me, until I felt a tap on my shoulder. "Get ready," warned the show's director, "because you and Zoe are on next."

CHAPTER TWELVE

MESS UP, MESS DOWN

I peeked out from behind the curtain. I looked at the stage, at the cameras.

I felt my knees shake. And for once, I wished I was more like Zoe—perfect.

I looked at her. But something was wrong.

"Do you know what it's like when everyone expects you to be perfect?" asked Zoe.

"No," I said, spotting a tear rolling down her cheek. "But no one really expects you to be perfect."

"Well, I do. And it's impossible!"

"Because nobody's perfect," I said.

Zoe looked at me funny.

"I'll try," said Zoe. She straightened her
shoulders. Her face turned serious. "So are you
ready, Guy?"

I nodded.

"And him?" She pointed at Peanut.

I tightened his helmet and parachute. "Yep."

"And what about me?"

"You?" I asked.

"Yes, how do I look?"

I looked at Zoe's silky pink dress, at her neatly combed hair, at the smile on her face. "You look—"

"Like a star?"

I nodded. Then I watched Zoe step onto the stage between the hamster cage and Tank's pizza tower (which was still leaning).

I stuffed the toy hamster into my pocket, held Peanut in one hand and his twitching nose with the other, and headed toward the ladder. Unfortunately, I had to let go of his nose to climb. And that's when he began to sniff…and shake.

But I held him tight.

I climbed up and up and up (without looking down) until I reached the top of the ladder. But just when things seemed to be going well—

I heard the **CRASH!**

I heard the **AAUGH!**

I looked down and saw the pizza tower splattered across the floor—and across Zoe's brand-new dress! And that's when I got dizzy, tightened my grip on the ladder…and loosened my grip on Peanut.

WHOOSH!

UH—OH!

Like a speeding bullet, Peanut shot out of my hand. He floated down, down, down, straight toward

I was dizzy and couldn't watch. But I heard Zoe's sirenlike scream. And as I climbed down the ladder, I heard the thumps, the yelps, the crashes. It sounded like an earthquake hit. Which is what the stage looked like when I finally stepped onto the ground. Everything was in a heap—tables, props, students, and even Miss Lizzy.

NOT A CREATURE WAS STIRRING . . .

. . . EXCEPT A PIZZA-MUNCHING HAMSTER.

Slowly, Miss Lizzy wobbled to her knees and looked into the still-running TV camera. "And that, boys and girls," she said, pointing to the mess around her, "is gravity."

She smiled.

Someone laughed.

Someone else laughed.

I laughed.

Miss Lizzy laughed.

Finally, even Zoe laughed.

Then the director yelled, "Cut!"

THE BARKER

Rockyville Elementary School News

CLASS HITS TV

Thursday's *The Super Science Show* was a "smash" hit, thanks to the final crashing demonstration of gravity by Miss Lizzy's class. "During the show, everything fell together," explained Miss Lizzy. "And at the end of the show, everything fell...together!"

TOWER TUMBLES

It is still a mystery as to why Tank's pizza tower fell and caused the show's messy ending. "Maybe someone pulled the string attached to the tower," said a still-angry Zoe.

"Or maybe it was blown over by the wind," replied Tank with a suspicious grin when asked if he knew what had happened.

VOICES IN THE CROWD

I WONDER IF THE DIRECTOR THINKS I LOOK LIKE A STAR.

Zoe

IT FEELS GOOD TO HAVE MY FEET BACK ON THE GROUND.

AND TO HAVE A FULL TUMMY.

Guy   Peanut

FOR ONCE I HAD NOTHING TO DO WITH THE MESS.

ME, NEITHER.

Zapper   Ollie

I HAVE NO IDEA HOW THE PIZZA TOWER FELL.

Tank

COMIC GUY

REMEMBER WHEN YOU SAID THAT NOTHING'S PERFECT?

YES.

WELL, YOU WERE WRONG.

BECAUSE THE SHOW'S ENDING WAS A PERFECT DISASTER.

GUY MALONEY

CHAPTER THIRTEEN
THE END OF WHO?

Thursday's TV show ended in a big mess. That's why we all decided to cheer up Miss Lizzy by making Friday an apple day.

Miss Lizzy was speechless. She was also hidden behind the pile of apples when she sat at her desk (and couldn't see that I was working on a comic strip).

"I love apples," said Miss Lizzy. She stood in front of the classroom and pointed at us. "And I love every one of you. Which is why I need to tell you—"

"That one of us is going be a cast member on *The Super Science Show*?" interrupted Zoe.

Miss Lizzy smiled. "Actually, someone from the class did make it."

"Then who?" asked Zoe.

"Peanut."

"The hamster?"

"I bet they'll pay him in pizza slices," I joked.

Miss Lizzy chuckled. "The director said Peanut brought excitement to the show."

"And disaster," snarled Zoe as she slumped in her chair. "I can't believe that rat is going to be a star."

"And so are you, Zoe," I said. "And so am I...in my comic strip." I showed her what I was working on.

But Zoe didn't laugh . . . or smile . . . until she finally realized that Peanut being on the TV show meant Peanut would be gone from the classroom.

I laughed. Then I looked up at our teacher. "What about you, Miss Lizzy?" I asked. "Did they offer you a job on the TV show?"

"Yes," she answered.

"To be the new Sciencewoman?"

"Yes."

Several students groaned. Tank slammed his fist on his desk. My stomach suddenly felt sick.

"But I turned them down," said Miss Lizzy.

"You did? Why?"

"Because I love teaching. And to me, teaching means being with students, answering their questions, and helping them understand by making science fun."

She taped a big yellow *S* on the front of her

lab coat and hopped on top of her desk. "So I'm staying here, and I will be *your* Sciencewoman!" She leaped into the air and landed in a heap on the floor.

The classroom exploded—in applause. Then Miss Lizzy rose to her feet and smiled like a star.

"It's a perfect ending," I said.

"You mean an almost-perfect ending," corrected a smiling Zoe.

And she was right. For the first time in a week, science class was back to normal. Kids sat on the edge of their seats, wondering what our nutty teacher would do next. I worked on a comic strip, knowing there were more funny ideas to come. And Miss Lizzy tried one of her crazy experiments, mixing two funny-colored liquids together, and—

CREATING COMIC STRIPS the COMIC GUY way

Lesson Two: **MAKING IDEAS FUNNY**

💡 You make ideas funny by thinking funny.

AND HOW DO YOU THINK FUNNY, GUY?

MY IDEAS
1. Cafeteria leftovers.
2. Crowded hallways.
3. Taking tests.

FIRST, I PICK AN IDEA, LIKE TAKING TESTS. THEN...

Ⓐ I **WRITE DOWN KEY WORDS**.

long tests   facts   too full
filling my head   explode

Ⓑ I **SKETCH**.

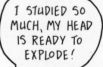

I STUDIED SO MUCH, MY HEAD IS READY TO EXPLODE!

Ⓒ I **EXAGGERATE**.

RATS! ANOTHER LONG TEST!

Ⓓ I **IMAGINE** THE **UNEXPECTED**.

Ⓔ I **ADD A TWIST**.

To do well on tests, you need to learn to think. To create good comic strip ideas, you need to learn to think funny. And you can do it — by practicing. Try it and see.

Learn more about creating comic strips by reading **Lesson Three**: "Drawing Funny Pictures" found in **COMIC GUY** Book #3.

About the Author/Illustrator

Timothy Roland likes to experiment. In science class, he used to experiment to see how long he could draw funny pictures before being caught by his teacher. (Usually, not very long!)

Today, Timothy still draws funny pictures and writes funny stories. "Which is like doing an experiment," he explains. "Because I pour my characters together and into crazy situations. I mix things up. And the result is usually an explosion—and a funny story for my new book series, **COMIC GUY**."

COMING SOON:

COMIC GUY #3
KOOKS IN THE CAFETERIA

"So I'm off the hook?" I asked, smiling.
"Not exactly. You're still guilty. But because of the circumstances, I don't think detention would be the appropriate punishment."
I let out a sigh of relief.
"Instead, I'm sentencing you to KP duty."
"Huh?" I said.
"One week of working in the school kitchen!"